NICOLE'S
BIRTHDAY

NICOLE'S BIRTHDAY

by Maud Frère

Illustrated by Nadine Forster
Translated from the French by Robin Gottlieb

Random House   New York

My dog Boniface rushed into my room this morning, licking my face and barking hello the way he always does. Only today he was wearing a big blue ribbon on which Mama had written "Happy Birthday!"

Then Papa came in to kiss me before leaving for the office. He gave me a wonderful box of paints. He sat on my bed and said, "Nicole, you must promise that from now on you'll finish your drawings. You do very nice things, but you have one big fault: You never finish what you start."

Papa is right. I went to the special drawer where I keep things I haven't finished, and when I opened it I saw all sorts of things I'd forgotten about. There was part of a sweater I was knitting for my doll Augustine, a handkerchief I once started to embroider for Mama's birthday, and a great heap of drawings I never finished.

For my birthday Mama gave me a big drawing pad, a pencil, and a red eraser.

Mama put on her best party dress. She said, "Aunt Augusta and Uncle Jules and your cousin Odilon are coming to lunch. Your twin cousins are coming too, and your little friend Arlette."

I clapped my hands and asked, "Will they bring me presents?"

"Don't ask questions like that any more, Nicole," Mama said. "You're a big girl now."

"What is a birthday exactly?" I asked her.

"It's the day of the year when you were born."

"And before that?" I asked. "Where was I before I was born?"

"In my heart," said Mama. "I always dreamed of having a little girl like you. You lived in my dreams."

It's funny to think that before I was born I lived in Mama's dreams. I guess all you have to do is dream of something and then it will become real!

Take Santa Claus, for example. In school that nasty Ginette told me that Santa Claus doesn't really exist. I asked Mama about it, and she said, "Santa Claus exists in our dreams. If he doesn't exist for Ginette, it's only because she doesn't believe in him."

"But does Santa Claus *really* exist?" I asked Mama.

"When you close your eyes, you see him, don't you?"

"Yes, of course," I said.

"And on Christmas Eve, you hear him on the roof, don't you?"

"Oh, yes," I said. "I heard him very clearly last year."

"Well, then," said Mama, "Santa Claus exists inside you, and that's what counts."

"Do *you* believe in Santa Claus, Mama?" I asked her.

"He lives in *my* dreams, too," she said.

Odilon, who is first in his class at school and knows geography, laughed at me when I told him what Mama said about Santa Claus.

"I never heard anything so silly in my life!" he said. "How can a dream be real?"

Well, that's Odilon. He loves to eat and is always stuffing himself with candy. For him, candy is real. But you can't eat a dream, so for him a dream isn't real.

Arlette was the first to arrive at my birthday party. She brought me a beautiful picture book. We went up to my room so I could show her the presents Papa and Mama gave me. Then we opened the drawer where I keep my secrets. She and Mama are the only ones who know about this drawer.

I keep all my most important things in this drawer. There are my diary and my best drawings, the seashells that I found on the beach last summer, a necklace Arlette strung for me, and my piggy-bank. Actually, I'm not very fond of the piggy-bank, but Mama says it's important to learn how to save money.

The next ones to arrive were my cousins Claude and Pierre. They're twins, and they look so much alike that you can hardly tell them apart.

They brought me a box of chocolates, which they held out to me proudly. A two-pound box, and I'm not allowed to have chocolate! I love it, but I can't have it.

I thanked the twins and tried to look pleased because I didn't want to hurt their feelings. Then Mama whisked away the box. She saw how disappointed I was (she sees everything), so she whispered in my ear, "Next Thursday we'll go into town, just the two of us, and have ice cream."

I love to go places with Mama and I love ice cream.

I did my best to smile at the twins and look happy, but underneath I was really a bit angry because every year they make the same mistake.

For ever so long I've been telling the twins that my doctor has strictly forbidden me to eat chocolate. They seem to be listening, and they nod their heads at me. Then I think, "This time they surely understand." But the twins must have wax in their ears or something, because each year on my birthday they come bringing chocolates again.

Mama always makes me give the chocolates to Mr. Plume, the poor old man who lives next door to us. Mr. Plume is very polite, and he always says, "Oh, no, Nicole, candy is for little girls like you."

But I insist. I say, "Please take them, Mr. Plume. Chocolate is like poison to me."

I see his eyes shining. He's all alone in the world, and Mama told me that nobody ever gives him presents. "You've made him very happy," Mama says later. Then I'm happy too, even happier than if I'd been able to eat the chocolates myself.

The twins are always very well dressed. They both have red bow ties, and they have their school emblem on their jackets.

Arlette likes them very much, but she can never tell one from the other. She claims she likes Pierre better—but when she thinks she's talking to Pierre she's really talking to Claude.

Finally Odilon and his family came, and there was a lot of shouting and kissing.

Uncle Jules, Odilon's father, is very boring, but Mama says I must be kind to him because he's a sick man.

Aunt Augusta is nice enough, but her nose is so terribly long. One day I was sent to bed early just because of her nose. I put my hand up to hide part of it, and I said, "You'd really look much better with just half your nose, Aunt Augusta." And whack! Mama gave me a slap and sent me straight off to bed.

That night I cried, because Mama told me how unhappy Aunt Augusta is about her long nose.

Uncle Jules gave me a present as boring as he is himself. He took a bill out of his wallet and said, "Here. For your piggy-bank."

I said, "Oh, thank you, Uncle Jules!" but I was very disappointed. I was hoping to get a red pencil box. Oh, well!

There! Everybody had come at last, and we all sat down to lunch. The grownups made a lot of noise talking and laughing. But we children had to be quiet, because Uncle

Jules hates noise. Odilon kept pinching me under the table to make me laugh, and the twins talked about football in whispers.

Finally the birthday cake was brought in. With one breath I blew out all the candles. I was so proud!

After lunch we played pirates in the attic. It was thrilling. We made two empty crates into beautiful boats, using broom handles for masts and sheets for sails. Arlette and I were in Pierre's boat. He was dressed up as a king, and we were his daughters. Odilon and Claude were the pirates, and they decorated their ship with skull-and-crossbones pictures.

We sailed along yelling, "Sail ho! Port and starboard! Ship ahoy!"

Odilon yelled the loudest. He has a voice that can pierce your eardrums. When we told him so, he claimed that pirates yell like that because they're strong. Maybe he's right, but his yells still hurt my ears.

The pirates had a hard time boarding our ship, because we fought very bravely. Finally, though, we were taken prisoner. The pirates tied us up and put us in the hold, with nothing to eat but bread and water.

Then, during the night while the pirates were sleeping, we climbed up on deck and tried to tie *them* up. According to the rules of the game, they should have let themselves be captured. But Odilon always cheats. He can't help it—it's just that he can never bear to lose. If he doesn't win every time, he grumbles. So when we tried to capture him, he really struggled. He hit out at us, yelling that we had no right to take the pirates prisoner because they were stronger than we were.

I got very angry, and Odilon and I had a real fight. He's much bigger and heavier than I am, of course, so he had me down in no time.

But I managed to grab one of the skull-and-crossbones pictures, and I brought it down over Odilon's head. It didn't hurt
him, but it made him feel very foolish. First he just stared at me
without moving a muscle. Then he let out his long shrill yell—the
yell that makes him turn blue and always brings his mother
running.

"Sore loser!" I said angrily. "Crybaby!"

Then Aunt Augusta arrived on the scene, followed by the
whole family. Odilon gave *his* version of what had happened, and
Aunt Augusta comforted her "dear, sweet little boy."

"Your daughter is a terrible roughneck!" Aunt Augusta said
to Mama. And they made us come downstairs because they said
we weren't able to play together without fighting.

For the rest of the after-
noon Odilon stayed near his
mother, being very quiet
and well behaved. Arlette
and I played lotto. Every so
often Odilon looked at us,
and when he did we made
faces at him. He pretended
not to notice and turned
away scornfully.

When it was time for him to leave, Odilon said good-by to me very coldly. I kissed him, and I also pinched his ear, which is a secret sign we have. It means, "Let's make up. I still like you."

But Odilon left without making up. He was really angry. I think it was because he made such a fool of himself in front of Arlette!

Still, all in all, it was a very nice birthday party.